Isla of Adventure
CITY PALS

by Dela Costa   illustrated by Ana Sebastián

LITTLE SIMON
New York London Toronto Sydney New Delhi

If you purchased this book without a cover, you should be aware that this book is stolen property. It was reported as "unsold and destroyed" to the publisher, and neither the author nor the publisher has received any payment for this "stripped book."

This book is a work of fiction. Any references to historical events, real people, or real places are used fictitiously. Other names, characters, places, and events are products of the author's imagination, and any resemblance to actual events or places or persons, living or dead, is entirely coincidental.

LITTLE SIMON
An imprint of Simon & Schuster Children's Publishing Division
1230 Avenue of the Americas, New York, New York 10020
First Little Simon paperback edition May 2024
Copyright © 2024 by Simon & Schuster, LLC
All rights reserved, including the right of reproduction in whole or in part in any form.
LITTLE SIMON is a registered trademark of Simon & Schuster, LLC, and associated colophon is a trademark of Simon & Schuster, LLC. For information about special discounts for bulk purchases, please contact Simon & Schuster Special Sales at 1-866-506-1949 or business@simonandschuster.com.
The Simon & Schuster Speakers Bureau can bring authors to your live event. For more information or to book an event contact the Simon & Schuster Speakers Bureau at 1-866-248-3049 or visit our website at www.simonspeakers.com.
Series designed by Laura Roode.
Book designed by Laura Roode.
The text of this book was set in Congenial.
Manufactured in the United States of America 0324 LAK
2 4 6 8 10 9 7 5 3 1
Cataloging-in-Publication Data is available for this title from the Library of Congress.
ISBN 978-1-6659-5040-4 (hc)
ISBN 978-1-6659-5039-8 (pbk)
ISBN 978-1-6659-5041-1 (ebook)

Contents

Chapter 1	A New Kind of Adventure	1
Chapter 2	Girls Trip!	13
Chapter 3	Much Like a Bird	25
Chapter 4	La Ciudad	35
Chapter 5	Pastries and Pigeons	47
Chapter 6	No Birds Allowed	57
Chapter 7	Small Bird, Big Problems	65
Chapter 8	Shop Til Your Feathers Drop	79
Chapter 9	Rat Attack!	91
Chapter 10	Friendship Pretzels	105

CHAPTER 1

A NEW KIND OF ADVENTURE

◆◆◆◆◆◆◆◆◆◆◆◆

Isla Verde typically began her days with a few important tasks.

The first task was brushing her hair and teeth at the same time. This way both chores went by faster.

Next, Isla made her bed with one quick pull of her blankets. Her gecko best friend, Fitz, helped by fluffing the pillows.

After that, Mama always whipped up a delicious breakfast for all three of them.

But today things were running a bit differently in the Verde house.

This time Isla wasn't following her usual routine. This time she was getting ready for her biggest adventure yet.

Today Isla was going on her first-ever airplane ride! All she had left to do before leaving the house was close her suitcase. But it turned out that filling it with clothes, books, and lots of adventure gear was making her suitcase a bit difficult to zip up.

Fitz watched from the couch as Isla fought with the zipper. "You're not moving to La Ciudad, you know. You crammed too much in there!" he said.

La Ciudad—the big city. It's where Mama had grown up, where Isla's friend Tora had moved from, and the one place Isla was most curious about.

"Crammed too much? No such thing!" Isla declared. Using both her hands, she tried to force the suitcase shut. "This old thing just needs . . . a little . . . push!"

"Allow me!" Fitz said. With one great gecko leap, he landed on the suitcase.

With the weight of her hands and Fitz's hops, the zipper finally gave in.

Ziiiiiiiiip!

Isla high-fived her friend. "This suitcase is as snug as a bug."

Fitz tilted his head. "Do you think you'll find bugs in La Ciudad? What if they're different than the ones here? What if they're super giant?"

Isla thought about it. The big city was, well, *big*.

"I haven't read anything about giant city bugs," Isla said, then gave Fitz a sad look. "But I do wish you could come find out with me."

Geckos weren't allowed on airplanes. It was the greatest bummer in the whole world.

"Me? In the sky? Hundreds of feet above the ground?" Fitz shivered. "That's no place for a gecko. You'll just have to draw everything you see and show me when you get back."

"It's a done deal," Isla promised.

The front door opened, and Mama walked in. She wore a pretty dress with a big sun hat. "Isla, is Fitz ready to head over to Abuelo's for the weekend? There are lots of sweet fruits that need to be picked from the garden. Plus, we've got a plane to catch!"

Fitz's stomach growled. "I don't know about picking the fruit, but I sure can eat it!"

Isla couldn't drag her suitcase out the door fast enough.

GIRLS TRIP!

◆◆◆◆◆◆◆◆◆◆◆◆◆◆

When Isla and Mama arrived at the airport, Isla wasn't sure what to expect.

Everyone said airports were gateways to new places. They sounded absolutely magical.

But when they stepped inside the large building, Isla raised her eyebrows. There were screens on walls and desks. Everyone seemed to be in a rush.

And there's wasn't a single Sol critter crawling around.

"It's so clean in here," Isla whispered to Mama. "Even the *floors* are sparkling."

She looked back to make sure her shoes hadn't left muddy tracks.

"Well, it's not the rain forest," Mama agreed. "But you'll have a blast all the same. You'll see."

Isla narrowed her eyes, trying to find the adventure. But all she saw was a blur rushing toward her and pulling her into a hug.

"Oof!" Isla huffed, letting go of her suitcase.

"Isla! You made it, you're here!" came the familiar squeal of Tora Rosa's voice.

Tora was Isla's friend and neighbor. It had been her idea to visit La Ciudad, and luckily, Mrs. Rosa and Mama had agreed it was a great idea. Tora also happened to be the only person who knew that Isla could speak with animals.

"I hope you haven't been waiting too long for us," Mama said to Mrs. Rosa.

Mrs. Rosa waved a hand. "Not at all! Are you excited, Isla?"

Isla hugged herself. "I have a million fireflies fluttering in my belly!" she said.

Tora laughed, then thought better of it. She slid down her heart-shaped sunglasses to look at Isla's belly. "Wait . . . you're joking, right?"

Isla winked. "Don't worry. All fireflies will remain here on Sol."

◊◊◊◊◊◊◊◊◊◊◊◊◊◊

The airport was a very busy place.

First, they needed to get their boarding passes from a lady at the ticket counter. As each pass printed out, she circled a number on the top corner.

"You'll need to go to gate twelve," she said. "That's where your airplane will be waiting."

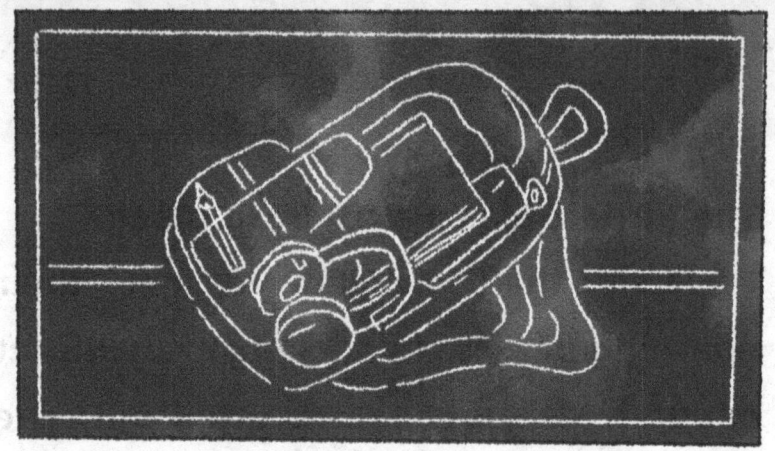

But before they could find their plane, everyone had to put their backpacks through a giant machine. It looked like an X-ray.

After they collected their belongings, it was time to search for gate twelve.

Isla couldn't believe how many shops were inside the airport: coffee shops, keychain stands, bookstores, and even restaurants.

"This place is giant! It's as big as the marketplace!" Isla exclaimed.

Gate twelve was between a sweets shop and a store that sold fruit bowls. They arrived just as the other passengers were lining up to have their boarding passes scanned. One by one, a woman at a podium scanned the passes.

Isla's turn came. Her hands were sweaty. What if her boarding pass didn't work? Would everyone have to stay behind because of her? What if—

BEEP!

The woman scanning Isla's pass smiled. "Welcome to your flight! Come on board."

CHAPTER 3

MUCH LIKE A BIRD

◊◊◊◊◊◊◊◊◊◊◊◊◊

"This. Is. Amazing," Isla whispered to Tora.

Travel notebook in hand, Isla sketched as she walked down the cabin aisle. The cabin was where all the passengers sat during the flight. Each seat was numbered and assigned.

"It's just like a bus," Isla added, still whispering. "But for the air."

Isla drew a man placing a small bag underneath the seat in front of him.

"Why are you whispering?" Tora asked. "It's a plane, not a library."

"I don't know," Isla admitted. "Maybe because this feels like a dream, and I don't want to wake up yet."

When they reached their assigned seats, Tora nudged Isla. "I think you should sit by the window," she said. "It's *my* favorite seat, but it's *your* first time flying."

"Are you sure?" Isla asked.

Tora shrugged. "If anyone wants to feel like a bird in the sky, I think it's you."

She's not wrong about that, Isla thought.

They settled into the seats, Mrs. Rosa and Mama right behind them.

Isla stared out the window. Right now all she could see were the outside parts of the airport. But soon Isla would see nothing but the clear blue sky.

"Good morning, travelers! This is your pilot, Captain Díaz, speaking," a voice said through the speakers. "Welcome to your nonstop flight to La Ciudad. Please make sure to fasten your seat belts."

Isla and Tora strapped theirs on. *Click!*

"Now sit back, relax, and enjoy the ride," the pilot said.

Tora squealed. "Take-off time!"

Outside the window Isla watched as the plane began to move. The world outside blurred by faster and faster. With a quick tilt, they were flying up into the sky.

Cotton candy-soft clouds flew by the window. Isla couldn't even see Sol anymore!

"We're in the sky!" Tora cheered. "How do you feel?"

Isla grinned. "Much like a bird."

LA CIUDAD

◊◊◊◊◊◊◊◊◊◊◊◊◊

Though they were high in the sky, that didn't mean there was nothing to do.

Much to Isla's surprise, there were tiny TVs attached to the backs of the airplane seats.

"Let's watch a movie," Tora suggested.

There was a mesh pocket below the screen with earphones wrapped in a baggie.

First, they watched a movie about a princess and a frog prince. That was Tora's favorite.

"There's no such thing as frogs that can turn into humans," Isla pointed out.

"Of course there's such a thing," Tora said, pointing to her head. "In here!"

Next, they watched a movie all about space. This one Isla *really* liked.

"People can't just go to space," Tora said.

"Of course they can!" Isla said. "You just have to train for it."

Halfway through the flight, Tora fell asleep while following a maze in her coloring book.

Giggling, Isla pulled out her notebook from her backpack and sketched her sleepy friend.

Not much later, the airplane's speakers switched on again.

"Hello, passengers," Captain Díaz said. "We will now be landing at La Ciudad Airport. The weather is clear and sunny, so we hope you get out there and enjoy your day."

"We're landing!" Isla squealed.

Tora jolted awake, swiping away at her drool. "Finally!"

The airplane flew lower and lower, until they safely reached the ground.

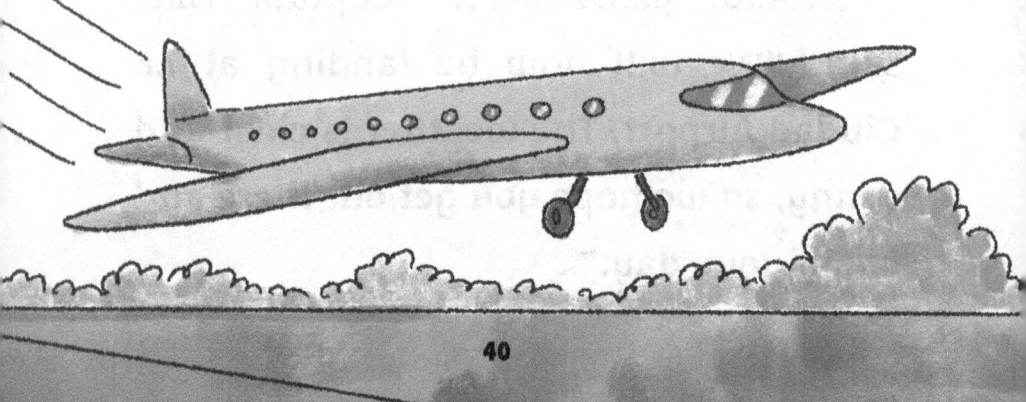

◆◆◆◆◆◆◆◆◆◆◆◆

Once they had found their suitcases, Isla followed Mrs. Rosa out the airport's sliding doors. There were lots of cars picking up other travelers. Mrs. Rosa raised her hand, and a yellow taxi pulled up right beside them.

"Can you take us to the hotel on Main Street?" she asked the driver.

"Sure thing!" the driver replied.

They piled into the taxi. As it drove off, Isla looked out the window in wonder.

Tall buildings glittered under the sun. The sidewalks were crowded with people. There were food carts lined up on the street. But it was the blue ocean on the horizon that made Isla gasp.

In some ways the city was just like her home island. Isla took out her notebook again and sketched the many sights. She could hear the sound of far-away seagulls and an upbeat jazz band marching along.

When the taxi arrived at the hotel, Isla's mouth dropped open. It was the biggest building she'd ever seen!

"Let's drop our things off," Mama said. "And then head out into the city!"

PASTRIES AND PIGEONS

◆◆◆◆◆◆◆◆◆◆◆◆◆

There was so much to do in La Ciudad, Isla was amazed. Everywhere she looked, something bright, exciting, and loud was happening.

Luckily, Tora was prepared.

"First things first," Tora said. "We have to buy matching La Ciudad T-shirts. It's a must!"

"That sounds good to me," Isla said.

With their moms, their first stop was a store made of yellow bricks. It had all sorts of La Ciudad gifts and trinkets.

The matching T-shirts were easy to find. Tora's had lots of pigeons on them. Isla also found a bag that read I ♥ LA CIUDAD.

As they hopped from store to store, Isla couldn't stop looking at all the glowing signs. It really was amazing how much there was to look at and do.

Her nose helped pick out their next stop. A sweet, sugary scent made her pause on the sidewalk.

Sniffing, she asked, "What's that amazing smell?"

"That's the bakery," Mrs. Rosa said, pointing to a small shop with loaves of bread on display. "They're very famous for their banana pastries."

That was the perfect gift for Fitz! He loved all snacks, but bananas were his absolute favorite.

"Why don't you girls go ahead," Mama suggested. "We'll be right next door buying lunch."

"Come on!" Tora said.

Isla pushed open the bakery door. The smell was even more delicious inside. Bakers with tall white hats kneaded dough, iced cakes, and filled the bakery case with treats.

"Oooh, what's this?" Isla pointed to something that looked like a banana.

"Ah!" a baker said. "That's our famous berries-and-banana pastry. It's got jam inside and chunks of fruit."

Isla took out her coin purse. "We'll take one!"

Tora dug out her heart-shaped coin purse, too. "And a pink donut!"

"I'll pack it up for you," the baker said. She took their pastries to the back for packaging.

Ding!

Isla turned to see who had walked in, but didn't see anyone.

"Ahem," a voice said. "I can't see the bakery case with you standing there!"

Surprised, Isla turned to look again.

"Oh, feathers," the voice groaned. "I'm down here!"

Isla looked down.

A bird with gray feathers and a soft pretzel around his neck stood behind them. And his big eyes looked very, very annoyed.

CHAPTER 6

NO BIRDS ALLOWED

◊◊◊◊◊◊◊◊◊◊◊◊◊

"A pigeon!" Isla exclaimed. "My first La Ciudad animal friend! Hi! I'm Isla Verde."

Tora looked down and shrieked. "Eek!"

"Hello, Isla," the pigeon said. "Hi, Eek."

"Her name's Tora, actually," Isla said.

"Wait a tootin' second," the pigeon said, inching closer. He tilted his head to get a better look with one big eye. "How can you understand what I'm saying? You're a human kid!"

Isla waved her hand. "Oh, I can speak to all animals."

"I can't," Tora added. "But even I can tell you're staring at the bakery case hungrily."

The pigeon kicked his feet. "Now that you mention it . . ."

Just then, the baker returned with their wrapped goods. "Here you go, ladies—agh! It's that pretzel pigeon again. What have I told you? No birds allowed! Shoo, shoo!"

She ran out from behind the counter and ushered the pigeon out of the bakery.

"Hey! I have bird rights!" he said, hopping about. "I got things to buy, lady!"

Isla cracked a smile. "Looks like he might need some help," she whispered.

Tora grabbed their boxed pastries and nodded firmly. "We'll be going now."

"Come on, bud," Isla said to the pigeon.

"That's your bird?" the baker asked, surprised.

"Birds don't belong to anyone," Isla replied. "They're free as the wind."

The door to the bakery closed behind her with the baker still surprised.

Outside, the pigeon perched on a blue mailbox and scowled. "Why, the nerve! How dare she kick me out!"

Isla shrugged. "I don't think humans are used to animals ordering food."

"Yeah, I thought pigeons liked food from . . . well, from anywhere," Tora said, taking a bite of her donut.

"Any old junk won't do," the pigeon said, huffing and puffing. "I'll have you know I like yummy things! And besides, this isn't for me. But it's no use. . . . I'll never find something good enough for the Feast of Crumbs."

With a strong flap of his wings, the pigeon took off and disappeared into the jungle of buildings as Isla watched.

I didn't even get his name, she thought sadly.

SMALL BIRD, BIG PROBLEMS

◊◊◊◊◊◊◊◊◊◊◊◊◊

As Isla, Tora, and their moms toured a large park the next day, Isla couldn't stop thinking about the upset pigeon.

What did he need? What was the Feast of Crumbs? What kind of crumbs were feasted on?

Isla didn't have to wonder for long. They were walking to the rose garden when Tora gasped. "Isla, look!"

The pretzel-wearing pigeon was perched on a trash can, picking out random bits of trash.

Isla tugged on Mama's sleeve. "Can we go to that part of the park? It's for . . . um . . ."

"It's so Isla can draw more pictures for Fitz," Tora quickly finished.

Nice save! Isla thought.

"All right," Mama said. "But stay close."

"And don't forget to smell the roses," Mrs. Rosa added.

Isla and Tora took off across the paved path to where their grumbling pigeon friend was picking through the trash.

"Hi!" Isla greeted him with a wave. "It's good to see you again. We never got your name."

The bird snapped his head to the side, one large eye narrowing. "It's Hankward Grayfeathers. But you can call me Hank. Now, shoo!"

He went back to picking trash.

"Ick!" Tora said, avoiding the trash.

"I'm busy," Hank answered. "I have no time to take pictures with tourists."

"We want to help you," Isla quickly explained. "You seem to be worried about the Crumbling Feast."

"It's the Feast of Crumbs," Hank corrected her. "Thanks for reminding me about the doom I'm about to face. A crumb-filled doom, that is."

"Huh?" Isla replied.

Hank sighed. "See, Bread Lady brings us her homemade breadcrumbs every single day right here in this park. She lets us eat with her and never tells us to shoo! That's why we pigeons bring her a gift every month."

Isla clapped her hands together. "How sweet!"

"Yeah, yeah," Hank grumbled. "Last month, I brought her a smoothie. Got it right out of this trash here. It's the best place to find gifts, if you ask me. But as I was delivering my gift, I accidentally dropped it . . . on her lap."

"You dropped the smoothie on Bread Lady's lap?" Isla repeated, horrified.

"Yikes," Tora said. "Sounds like you need help impressing Bread Lady this time around."

Isla slammed a fist into her open hand. "Hank, we're going to help you find the perfect gift!"

Hank flapped his wings excitedly. "Say, that sounds like a nice idea! Where do we start?"

"Good question." Isla turned to Tora. "What do you say, city girl? Where should we go?"

Tora beamed. "The best thing about La Ciudad is that there are stores everywhere. Even right here in the park!"

Still, Hank was a pigeon and couldn't just fly into stores. He needed a place to hide.

Isla held open her bag. "Why don't you hang out in here?"

Hank shrugged. "I've been in worse places."

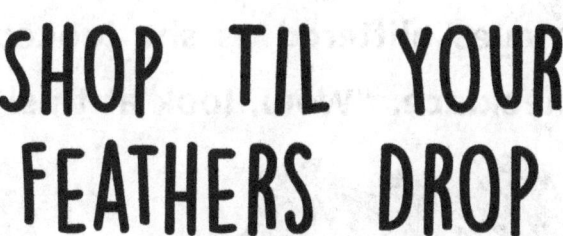

SHOP TIL YOUR FEATHERS DROP

◆◆◆◆◆◆◆◆◆◆◆◆◆

The first store in the park was filled with beautiful dresses and shoes.

"Oooh, this is nice," Hank said. "Look at all this human stuff!"

Isla picked up a large dress with lace. "This is nice, but . . . we don't know Bread Lady's size."

The next store they walked into was called La Ciudad Jewels.

It was filled with cases and cases of shiny necklaces, bracelets, and rings. Tora's eyes glittered as she looked at a pink necklace. "Wow, look at this!"

A saleswoman came forward. "Would you girls like to see this? It's only five hundred dollars."

Hank gulped. "Can we pay with empty coffee cups from the trash?"

It was best to move on somewhere else.

The next store was called City Gifts. It was filled with all sorts of pins, stickers, notebooks, and trinkets.

Isla plucked a pigeon-shaped cooking timer. "Look at this! It's cute."

Hank ducked into Isla's bag. "It's terrifying!"

"How about this cool cup?" Tora shook it and glitter floated inside. "It even comes with a straw."

"Oh, sure." Hank rolled his eyes. "So Bread Lady can remember the smoothie spill?"

"Definitely not!" Isla giggled.

Tora sighed, putting the cup back. "You are one picky pigeon."

Hank didn't like a silly bobblehead or a pen with rainbow ink. He *really* didn't like the T-shirt that said BEWARE THE PIGEONS. Just as they were thinking about giving up, Hank flew out of Isla's bag and landed on a counter with postcards.

"Wait a second," he said, pecking at the cards. "This here might do the trick."

"This one's nice," Tora said. She picked up a postcard with hearts all over city buildings.

Hank let out a happy coo. "This will show Bread Lady that I love sharing the city with her."

The girls put together the last of their coins and paid for the postcard.

Outside, they returned to Hank's trash can. He flew out of Isla's bag with the postcard in his beak.

In a flurry of happiness, Hank began wiggling around.

"Hank—are you dancing?" Tora asked.

"He's celebrating," Isla said, joining her pigeon friend in a dance. "He's going to have the best gift!"

Tora stared, shrugged, and broke out into a wiggling dance too.

"Oh yeah!" Hank said. "Do the pigeon dance!"

The postcard fell from Hank's beak and landed on the ground. A sudden gust of wind began to blow the card away.

"Grab it!" Tora cried.

The three raced to catch it, but the wind was quicker. With one final push, the postcard flew right into a storm drain.

"Oh, feathers!" Hank wailed.

RAT ATTACK!

◆◆◆◆◆◆◆◆◆◆◆◆◆

Isla and Tora peeked into the sewer. The card floated in green, murky water.

"Well . . . it's definitely stinky now." Isla pinched her nose. "One of us could reach in . . ."

Tora jumped back. "I don't think it's a good idea to put our hands in there."

Isla nodded. No one should stick their hand into mysterious openings.

"This is a job for the underground city," Hank said, pretending to roll up his sleeves.

"The underground city?" Isla echoed. "That sounds super cool."

"More like super icky," Tora said. "The underground city is what city folks call the sewers and the critters inside them."

"Here comes help now." Hank stuck his head into the drain. "Hey, you! Wanna help us out?"

Who's he talking to? Isla wondered.

That's when she spotted a small, furry rat with a long tail. She was busy sniffing the postcard.

"Wow!" Isla said, waving excitedly.

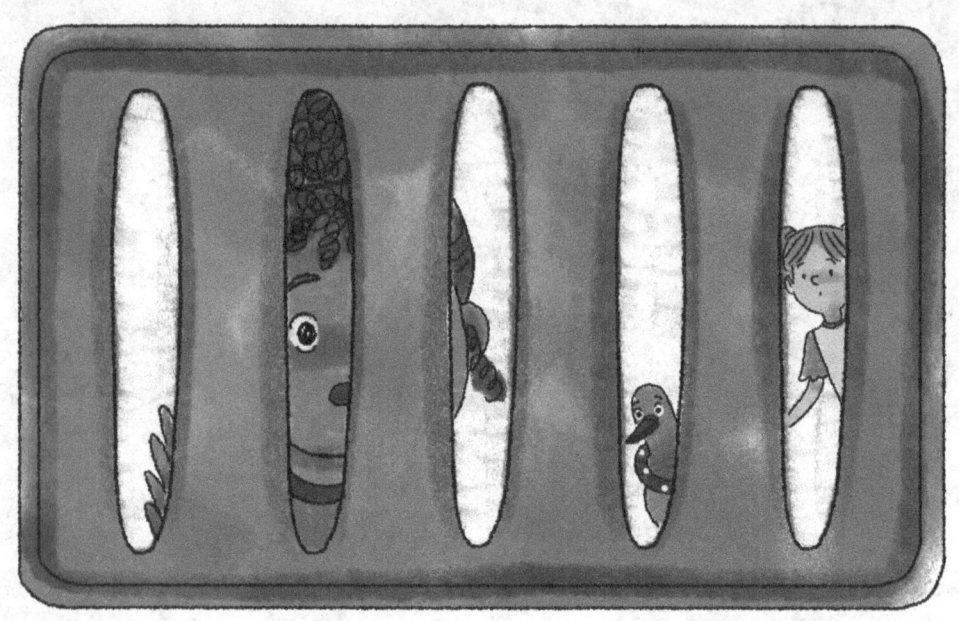

"Hi, there! Would you mind returning that card to us?"

"The quicker, the better!" Tora added.

The rat looked up with a glint in her eye. "You want this pretty thing back?"

"Yes, yes!" Hank said impatiently.

The rat snatched the postcard right

up. "No can do! See, whatever falls into the sewers belongs to us rats."

"But . . . but . . . ," Isla stammered.

"Sorry, kid. I'm a finder and a keeper," the rat hissed. "See ya!"

She scurried off into the dark.

"Hey! You owe us a few quarters for that!" Tora shouted into the sewer.

Hank let out a sudden cry, his wings covering his face. "Oh no—the Feast of Crumbs is starting! Look!"

Isla turned to face the opposite side of the park. A short-haired woman wearing a beautiful dress was sitting on a wide bench.

"Sweet friends!" she called out. "I've arrived!"

She reached into her purse and brought out a baggie filled with glazed breadcrumbs. As she tossed them out, pigeons appeared from all corners.

They flew down from trees, scurried out from bushes, and left behind other snacks. They cooed happily at the sight of Bread Lady.

"Whoa," Tora said. "They all have gifts."

Isla couldn't believe her eyes as pigeons dropped random knickknacks at Bread Lady's feet. She saw a half-eaten bagel, bracelets, and even seashells.

"Oh, how kind of you!" Bread Lady smiled.

"How did they find all of that?" Isla wondered aloud.

"Pigeons always find a way," Hank said glumly. "Except for me."

Isla and Tora shared a sad look. They couldn't stand seeing Hank so glum.

"Don't give up yet," Isla said. "We just need a back-up plan."

Tora looked through her backpack. "I have exactly one nickel, half my pink donut, and . . . that's it."

Isla searched her bag. It carried Fitz's souvenir, her empty coin purse, pencils, and her notebook.

"I'll find a gift," Hank cried out. "Oh, I need an emergency snack break."

He took a small bite of his pretzel necklace.

Isla's eyes narrowed. "Hank . . . why do you wear that around your neck?"

"This old thing?" he asked. "It's my favorite snack. Plus, it keeps me snug."

"It kind of looks like a friendship necklace," Tora said.

Isla gasped. "Tora! You're a genius!"

Tora blinked. "I am?"

"Yes!" Isla kneeled closer to Hank. "You should get Bread Lady a pretzel necklace of her own. That way, you'll be pretzel-bound best friends forever!"

FRIENDSHIP PRETZELS

◆◆◆◆◆◆◆◆◆◆◆◆

"Say, that's it!" Hank cooed happily. "That's just the thing!"

Without wasting another second, Hank flew to a nearby pretzel stand. There was a lone soft pretzel on the ground. He snatched it up and flew off toward Bread Lady.

Isla and Tora nervously watched Hank approach the other pigeons.

"Hank's here!" the pigeons whispered, curiously watching. "I can't believe he actually showed up."

"What's he gonna spill this time?" one grumbled.

Bread Lady paused in surprise as Hank landed on her lap. Gently, he slipped the pretzel around her wrist like a bracelet.

"Oooh, I can't look!" Tora squealed, covering her face. "Does she like it?"

"I can't tell yet," Isla replied.

On the bench, Bread Lady's eyes widened as she inspected Hank's gift. "Why . . . this . . . this is . . ."

All the pigeons leaned in. Isla held her breath. Tora peeked from between her fingers.

"This is wonderful! And it matches your lovely necklace," Bread Lady finally said. "We'll always be true friends."

Hank cooed and flew up to give her a peck on the cheek.

"He did it!" Tora celebrated, hugging Isla.

"Great job, Hank!" one pigeon cried out.

"Yeah!" another said. "Here, I saved you some crumbs."

Hank joined his friends, then waved happily at Isla and Tora.

◆◆◆◆◆◆◆◆◆◆◆◆◆◆◆

On the very last night of the trip, Isla and Tora sat at their own table in a fancy outside restaurant. Mama and Mrs. Rosa sat nearby, planning the return to Sol.

"Isn't this cool?" Tora exclaimed. "This must be what being a grown-up feels like."

A waiter came by to take their orders. Tora asked for a cheeseburger with fries, while Isla ordered cheesy ravioli.

The waiter scribbled down their orders and hurried off.

Tora took a sip of her lemonade, then squealed.

"What is it?" Isla asked. "Is your lemonade too sour?"

"Not exactly," Tora replied. "But there's something touching my leg under the table."

Curious, Isla slipped off her chair and lifted the tablecloth to see a pair of large eyes looking back at her.

"Hey, pal," Hank said.

"It's you!" Isla gasped in delight.

"It's who?" Tora asked, appearing underneath the table too. "Oh, Hank! What are you doing here?"

The pigeon blushed. "Well, I had to give you a proper thank-you, didn't I?"

"How was the rest of the Feast of Crumbs?" Isla asked.

Hank fluffed out his feathers. "Let's just say I'm Bread Lady's number one pigeon. But enough about me. I brought you something."

He stepped aside to reveal two small soft pretzels.

Tora gasped, pressing a hand to her heart. "Are those pretzel bracelets for . . . us?"

"Just a little gift," Hank said shyly. "Bread Lady isn't the only human who's been kind to me."

Isla felt warm all over with happiness. "This is so sweet of you, Hank."

"Go on, put them on! They're still warm from the pretzel cart," Hank said.

Isla grabbed one and passed the other to Tora. They slipped on their new bracelets and admired them.

Tora wiggled her wrist around. "I definitely don't have this in my jewelry collection."

"It's a Hank specialty," Hank cooed. "Well, I'm off! I heard it through the pigeon vine that Bread Lady is making a special appearance at the park. Get this— she's bringing extra crumbs tonight!"

"Before you go, Hank," Isla said, "could I sketch you in my adventure notebook?"

"Oh, you want a memory of good ol' Hank?" he asked, then struck a dramatic pose. "You got it, kiddo!"

Isla reached up to grab her notebook and began sketching. Tora giggled as Hank modeled, and Isla thought this might just have been her best adventure yet.

DON'T MISS ANY OF ISLA'S ADVENTURES!

If you like Isla's adventures, then you'll love...

the CRITTER club

EBOOK EDITIONS ALSO AVAILABLE from LITTLE SIMON
CritterClubBooks.com